TREVOR

Based on *The Railway Series* by the Rev. W. Awdry

Illustrations by
Robin Davies and Jerry Smith

EGMONT

EGMONT

We bring stories to life

First published in Great Britain 2005
by Egmont Books Limited
239 Kensington High Street, London W8 6SA

Thomas the Tank Engine & Friends

A BRITT ALLCROFT COMPANY PRODUCTION

Based on The Railway Series by The Rev W Awdry

© Gullane (Thomas) LLC 2005

ISBN 1 4052 1717 0
1 3 5 7 9 10 8 6 4 2
Printed in China

*T*his is a story about Trevor the Traction Engine. He was going to be broken up for scrap. But then he met Edward, who was determined to find his new friend a home....

The Fat Controller works his engines hard. But they are very proud when he calls them Really Useful.

"I'm going to the scrap yard today," Edward called to Thomas.

"What, already? You're not that old!" replied Thomas, cheekily.

Thomas was only teasing.

The scrap yard is full of rusty old cars and machinery. They are broken into pieces, loaded into trucks and Edward pulls them to the Steelworks, where they are melted down and used again.

There was a surprise waiting for Edward in the yard.

It was a traction engine.

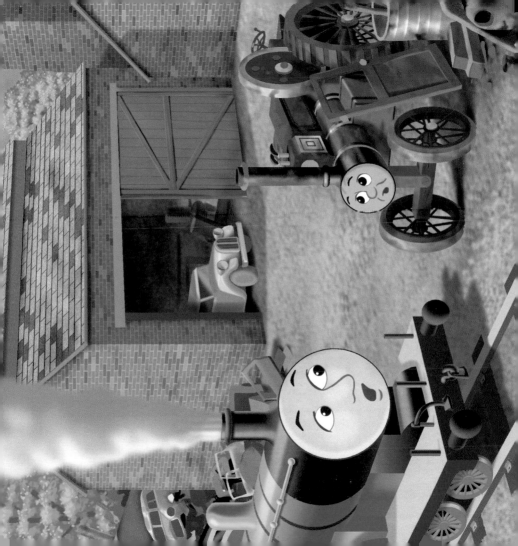

"Hello," said Edward. "You're not broken and rusty. What are you doing here?"

"I'm Trevor," said the traction engine, sadly. "They're going to break me up next week."

"What a shame," said Edward.

"My Driver says I only need some paint, polish and oil to be as good as new," continued Trevor. "But my Master thinks I'm old-fashioned."

Edward snorted. "Some people think I'm old-fashioned. But I don't care. The Fat Controller says I'm a Useful Engine."

"My Driver says I'm useful, too," said Trevor. "Even if a job is hard, I don't give up, and I've never broken down in my life."

"What work did you do?" asked Edward.

"My Master would send us from farm to farm," Trevor replied. "We threshed corn, hauled logs and did lots of other work. The children loved to see us."

Trevor shut his eyes – remembering …

"I miss the children," he sighed.

Edward set off for the station.

"Broken up – what a shame. Broken up – what a shame," he clanked. "I must help Trevor, I must."

Edward thought of all his friends who liked engines, but he knew none of them would have room for a traction engine at home!

"It's a shame. It's a shame," he hissed.

As Edward pulled into the station, there, standing on the platform, was the Vicar.

"Hello, Edward. You look upset," he said. "What's the matter, Charlie?" he asked Edward's Driver.

"There's a traction engine in the scrap yard, Vicar," the Driver replied. "He'll be broken up next week. Jem Cole says he's never driven a better engine."

"Do save him, Sir," said Edward. "He's a very Useful Engine – he can carry wood and give children rides."

"We'll see," replied the Vicar.

Jem Cole came to the scrap yard on Saturday.

"The Reverend is coming to see you, Trevor," he said. "Maybe he'll buy you."

"Do you think he will?" asked Trevor, hopefully.

"He will when I've lit your fire and cleaned you up," Jem told him.

The Vicar and his two boys arrived that evening.

"Show us what you can do, Trevor," said the Vicar.

Trevor chuffered around the yard. He hadn't felt so happy for months.

Later, the Vicar came out of the office smiling.

"Trevor is coming home with me, Jem," he said.

"Do you hear that, Trevor?" cried Jem. "The Reverend has saved you and you'll live at the vicarage now."

"Peep, peep!" whistled Trevor, happily.

Now Trevor's home is in the vicarage orchard and he sees Edward every day.

His paint is spotless and his brass shines like gold.

Trevor likes his work, but his happiest day is the Church Fête.

With a wooden seat bolted to his bunker, he chuffers around the orchard, giving rides to children.

Long afterwards, you will see him shut his eyes – remembering . . .

"I like being with children again," he whispers, happily.

The Thomas Story Library is THE definitive collection of stories about Thomas and ALL his Friends.

5 more Thomas Story Library titles will be chuffing into your local bookshop in April 2006:

'Arry and Bert
George
Jack
Annie and Clarabel
Rheneas

And there are even more
Thomas Story Library books to follow later!

So go on, start your Thomas Story Library NOW!